MARCELLA'S

D1400129

PLAYHOUSE

TOOL
SHED

PLAYROOM

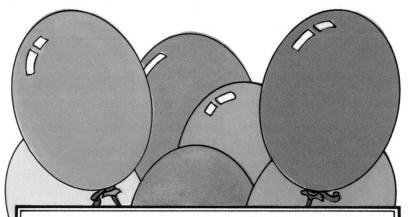

This book belongs to:

_____

Raggedy Ann & Andy's

GROW AND LEARN LIBRARY

VOLUME 11

THE JACK-IN-THE-BOX

A LYNX BOOK

This book is published by Lynx Books, a division of Lynx Communications, Inc., 41 Madison Avenue, New York, New York 10010. The name "Lynx" together with the logotype consisting of a stylized head of a lynx is a trademark of Lynx Communications, Inc.

Raggedy Ann and Andy's Grow-and-Learn Library, the names and depictions of Raggedy Ann, Raggedy Andy and all related characters are trademarks of Macmillan, Inc.

One morning, Marcella's cousin David came to visit.
David had brought a brightly colored tin box with him.
He set it on the floor in the playroom, right near Raggedy
Ann. Then he and Marcella sat on the floor to build a city
out of blocks.

"I wonder what's in this box," thought Raggedy Ann.
Raggedy Andy wondered the same thing. He wished
he could ask David to open it, but he knew he would have
to wait to find out what was inside.

"Maybe it's full of beautiful clothes," Babette the
French Doll thought hopefully.

Tim the Toy Soldier thought the box might be full of tiny toy soldiers that he could play with.

Raggedy Cat could hardly keep her paws still as she stared at the box. "I'll bet it's full of fluffy balls of yarn that I can bat across the floor," she thought happily.

Just as Marcella was placing the very last block on the tallest building in the city, her father called to her. "It's time to put the blocks away," he said. "We're ready to leave for the picnic."

"Hurray!" cried Marcella.

"Yea!" exclaimed David.

"Great!" thought Raggedy Andy. "As soon as they're gone, we can open the box."

"Hurry up," thought Tim as he watched the children stack the blocks neatly in a corner.

Finally, Marcella and David were ready to leave. David reached for his tin box.

Raggedy Andy almost cried out, "No! Don't take that with you!" But he caught himself just in time.

The dolls were all very happy when Marcella said,
"There will be so many things to do at the picnic, David.
Why don't you leave that here until we come back?"
The dolls were even happier when David agreed.

The dolls waited quietly until they heard the sound of the car pulling out of the driveway.

Then they gathered around the mysterious box. There was a handle on one side of it, and Raggedy Ann reached out and turned it.

"Just as I thought," she said as music filled the air. "It's a music box!"

"We already have a music box," said Raggedy Andy in a disappointed voice.

The words were barely out of his mouth when the lid sprang open and up popped a clown! The clown laughed as he watched all the dolls jump back in surprise.

"That's what you get for turning my handle without asking!" he said.

"I'm sorry," said Raggedy Ann. "I didn't know anyone lived inside the box. What is your name?"

"Jack, of course. Haven't you ever seen a jack-in-the-box before?" he asked.

The dolls shook their heads.

"Just because we've never heard of a jack-in-the-box doesn't mean we can't be friends!" said Bubbles the Clown Doll. Bubbles thought he and Jack might be especially good friends—since they were both clowns.

"Well, I'm not an everyday clown," sniffed Jack.

"Your clothes are beautiful," said Babette.

"And it must be nice to have your own built-in music," added Greta the Dutch Doll, hoping to make him feel welcome.

"It certainly is," said Jack. "It's just one of the things that's special about me."

"We love to have visitors in our playroom," Raggedy Ann told him. "We hope you like it here."

"This playroom's okay," said Jack. "But the room that I live in is much bigger than yours. And we have more dolls and toys to play with, too."

"We have nice things to play with," said The Camel with the Wrinkled Knees. "Would you like me to show you around?"

"No, thanks," Jack yawned. "I'd rather just take a nap." And he reached up and pulled down the lid, disappearing into his box.

"I don't think he wants to be our friend," said Babette. "I don't think so either," said The Camel sadly. "I guess he doesn't like us very much. Maybe our playroom isn't very special after all."

"Our playroom is just fine," said Raggedy Ann. "In fact, I think we should just leave Jack alone now and decide what we want to do while Marcella and David are gone."

"Anybody want to play circus?" asked Raggedy Andy.

"Great!" they all shouted.

"I'll be the ringmaster," said Percy the Policeman Doll. He blew his whistle and called out . . .

"Ladies and gentlemen and dolls of all ages! Come one, come all, to the greatest show in the playroom!"

Then Raggedy Andy tumbled across the floor in the most wonderful display of flips and twists and cartwheels and handsprings. Raggedy Andy took a bow, and all the other dolls clapped.

Inside the box, Jack was beginning to wonder what all
the noise was about.

"And now, in the center ring," shouted Percy, "we have Babette, our lovely animal trainer, and her fearsome feline, Raggedy Lion."

Babette stood on a little box and shouted commands at the make-believe lion. As all the dolls and toys watched, Raggedy Cat pawed the air. Then she let out the loudest roar ever to come out of such a tiny mouth.

Well, maybe it was more of a growl than a roar. But since none of the dolls had ever heard a real lion roar, no one knew the difference.

Everyone laughed and clapped for Raggedy Cat and Babette.

Jack peeked out of his box to see what was going on.

When the applause died down, The Camel with the Wrinkled Knees walked shyly into the spotlight.

"What would a circus be without an elephant?" asked Percy. "And it just so happens that we have here our very own 'Elephant with the Wrinkled Knees'!"

Moving very slowly, just like a real elephant, The Camel climbed onto the little box in the middle of the room.

Lifting his head up high, he gave the best imitation of a trumpeting elephant that had ever been heard from a toy camel.

Then, placing his two front legs upon the stool, he did a perfect handstand while Tim played his drum loudly.

"Hurray!" cried the dolls.

The Camel smiled shyly as he left the ring.

"Now welcome Greta," called Percy, "and her clever little pup, Raggedy Dog. Isn't he wonderful, folks?" Percy continued, as Raggedy Dog walked across the floor on his hind legs without missing a beat.

Then Greta the Dutch Doll held a hoop high above her head. Raggedy Dog jumped through it again and again as everyone cheered.

Raggedy Ann looked over at Jack. She saw he was watching the show with a very sad look on his face.

When Greta and Raggedy Dog finished their act, Raggedy Ann walked over to Jack's box.

"What's wrong?" she asked. "Don't you like our circus?"

"Well . . ." Jack began. "It's all right. I mean, I wish—"

"Hey!" shouted Raggedy Andy. "I think Jack wants to play with us after all!"

"I do!" Jack blurted out. "I'm sorry I wasn't nice to you before. But I was afraid you wouldn't like me. So I tried to pretend that I was better than everyone else. Now I guess nobody likes me very much."

Raggedy Ann smiled. "We thought *you* didn't like *us!*" she told him.

"I do like you," Jack said softly.

"Good!" said Raggedy Ann. "Then why don't you join us now?" she asked.

And that's just what Jack did.

"Do you think you'd like a little music for your circus?" Jack asked. He reached over to crank the handle on the side of his box.

"What perfect circus music!" said The Camel.
Jack kept turning the handle.

Percy blew his whistle.

"And now," cried Percy, "as Jack plays his musical box, it gives me great pleasure to present the rest of our show!"

Jack played the music as Babette twirled a tiny baton and pranced about the room. Tim marched right beside her, beating his drum to the music.

Bubbles the Clown did a funny little dance. Then he threw three little balls into the air and began to juggle.

Raggedy Ann was just about to pull flowers out of a hat in her magic act when they heard a car pulling into the driveway.

"Marcella is home!" announced The Camel.

"Quick, let's get everything cleaned up," said Raggedy Andy. And they quickly put everything away and got back in their places.

Jack scrunched himself down into his box. But before he closed the lid, he said, "That sure was a great circus! And thanks for giving me another chance."

"Anytime," answered Raggedy Andy. "It's always nice to have a new friend."

Raggedy Ann couldn't help noticing the big smile that spread across Jack's face just before he snapped his lid shut.

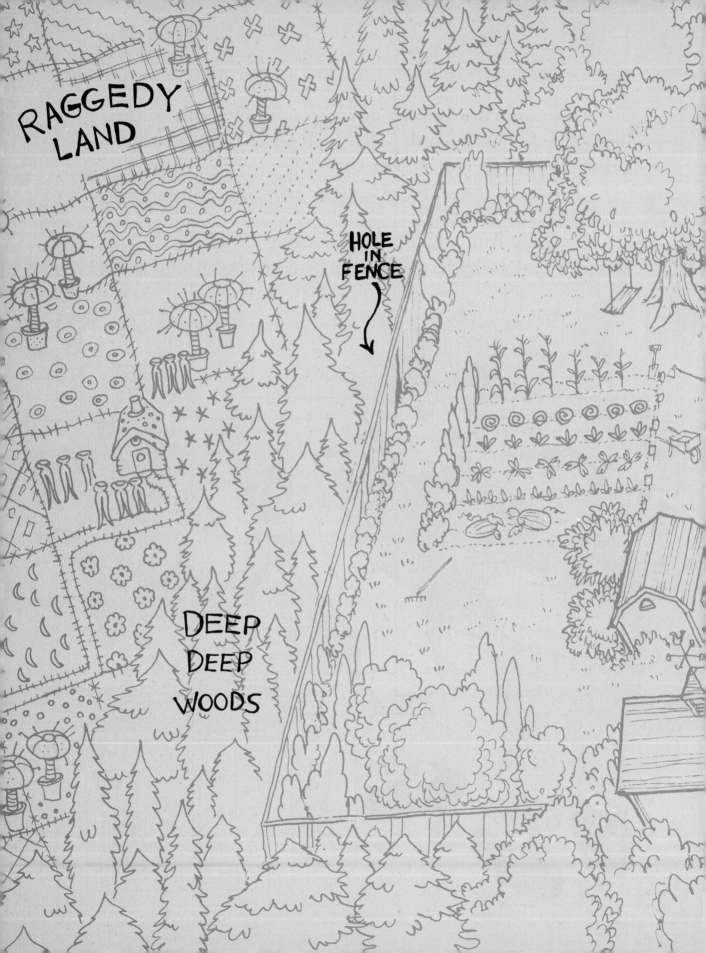